POWERLESS
PRISONERS

POWERLESS PRISONERS

Kenny McFadden

Library of Congress Control Number: 2023915784
ISBN: Hardcover   978-1-6698-9029-4
               Softcover   978-1-6698-9030-0
               eBook   978-1-6698-9031-7

Print information available on the last page.

Rev. date: 08/18/2023

To order additional copies of this book, contact:
Xlibris
UK TFN: 0800 0148620 (Toll Free inside the UK)
UK Local: (02) 0369 56328 (+44 20 3695 6328 from outside the UK)
www.Xlibrispublishing.co.uk
Orders@Xlibrispublishing.co.uk
854928

They could teach him how

To mix the mortar,

And how to lay the stones,

But If he didn't know

How to make the bricks,

How could he call this Place his home.

Contents

1

The Nostrils

"How many rims on your wheel would it take to sole my boots" Coinneach said to the lady sitting on the bench beside Ushet lake with her bicycle abandoned in the grass verge…

"Well now why should I care" said Maggi shifting her position, sliding to the edge of the bench tearing shards of green paint as she did so, leaving a space for the hiker in green work trousers sturdy walking boots and a maroon North Face anorak.

Coinneach sat down unsteadily and as he pulled out his black moleskin notebook from the inside pocket of his tan leather waistcoat said "Thankyou kindly lady"

He read the last paragraph

I haven't the faintest clue what your talking about, and you know whats more, it doesn't even bother me.

And with a well rehearsed movement put pen to paper

My comings and goings with the world in general, well they were. That was all

He sat with consciousness derailed and communicated with a calf. there would be no movement, no welcome or goodbye, only essential functions to enable his stand to be held. signs had been placed at generous distances from his position to remove his legitimacy of targeting by strangers or accomplices, only a faint whisper of the train was heard as he sat in the natural silence of a half dead dawn. an existence was no longer justifiable, others grasped for their place through the aside of friends, he for the wisdom inside, his own was growing restless for the funds to establish a retreat, an evenings solitude a peace a place to rest his soul a while. Old memories flicker and fade into the new vision, their place now established, the withdrawal in practice, the castle ruins windswept and torn, only now when the gatekeeper had been dislodged, could he enter through the façade and refocus.

Maggi cleared her throat and coughed as coinneach finished his writing and lifted her knapsack opening it halfway and lifting out a green stanley thermos continued to pour out the coffee into the cup.

Coinneach looked at Maggi she wore a trilby with her curly black hair sweeping down to her shoulders touching on her long red leather coat and calf high Doc Martens with yellow and black laces, she was curvy and he guessed she was in her late thirties.

"as I child I used to call girls smellies", he said.

"Oh, is that what you were writing?", she enquired before taking a sip of her coffee.

"No, not that but as opposed to holding your thoughts sacrosanct I have come to believe we should promote respect and question engagement with others and their journey through life, time and the ravages of self awareness and the jovial destruction of the life and the times of this ever isolating world.", Coinneach went on,

"I don't really want to talk about anything that I have to talk about and I'm not interested in anything anybody else had to say",

"Well then here's what I've written" Maggi said

as she pulled out a crumpled piece of paper placed

her cup on the bench and read in a jaunty tone :-

"I Sayeth Lace

A feather for a pillow, a flower for a

breath,

An alter made of sage and straw, alms

for a heart that yet

May beat the great resounding tone

In time to hear

I sayeth

An arctic wind of lace, from the breath

of the foxglove

To the spirit of dew, a candlelit vigil

In reverence of the view"

"so are you a writer as well?" coinneach said in a hopeful tone

"Well I don't call myself that but I do put pen to paper

sometimes", maggi said in a cheerful tone,

"I wrote that one here at Ushett yesterday".

"I loved the poem or prose whatever you may call it, it was great

easy on the ear and provocative."

"I'm a tailor by trade", Magi went on, "that's how I earn my living anyways",

"Me I'm a pipe layer, storm water and sewage pipes mostly work for Benny O'Neils Civils in Belfast"

"Do you live on the island or are you just visiting?" Coinneach asked

"just visiting" Maggi said as she finished her last sip of coffee, "and you?" she asked

"staying for a few months, how longs a piece of string really" coinneach replied

"Twice the length of half of it" maggi quipped,

"What?" coinneach said absently,

"twice the length of half of it, you asked how long is a piece of string", Maggi said looking pleased with herself.

"would you like a coffee?" maggi asked as she pulled out her green Stanley Thermos and poured herself another cup,

"I have some here of my own, but I'd try one of yours if that's okay, I'll pay you for it." Coinneach said excitedly, he loved his coffee and reckoned he had about 20 cups a day, hot or cold it didn't matter, he fumbled in his pocket and brought out a 2 pound coin and proffered it in maggi's direction, "keep your pride in your pocket" maggi laughed as she brought out a worn blue tin cup from her knapsack and poured half a cup before offering it over to coinneach.

The Angelus Bells rang out from the chapel, the call to prayer had coinneach reaching for his notebook and pen as he glanced at his watch 12 o'clock. He wrote for ten minutes or more as maggi closed her eyes and let the gusts of wind toss her hair and mixed with the sound of crows squawking and seagulls calling she relaxed into the atmosphere with all it's wildness and sea smells coming in from a mile away where a small rocky cove, bay was her destination for the day.

[In Between]

I thought I heard a chapel call,
In between the chimes.

It bled the fragrance of the day,
And held me close and rhymed.

It may have been a fleeting thought
A dream from bygone times.

But all I hold, close to me,

Is in between those chimes.

There was plenty of silences between the two as they sat there dishevelled by the wind and the odd skiff of rain that first time they met. Maggi caught up in thoughts about her work, her children and the need for a constant flow of income for the bills, schooling, food and the mortgage, but for the couple of hours they sat there she was immersed in the atmosphere and her ebb was refuelling her spirit soul and body. She had had a great week so far eating from the local café a mixture of salads cheese toasties and vegetable broth, and walking around the island taking in the peace and solitude and talking to the occasional holiday maker and local fishermen. Life had been hard these past few years yes bloody hard and she felt as if she was turning the corner, as if a change was coming. She just wanted to be running half clad, naked even through forests beside lakes and streams and commune with the gods chanting pagan prayers and seeing the signs that the gods sent by way of reward. She was a necromancer a spirit capable of casting spells and telling indeed influencing the future that was all she ever wanted to be.

A Spiritual Plinth

A sunset reveller, of professional hue,

With ornamental undertones,

In a droplet of dew,

Forsaking nothing, to abide,

In a moonlit dream of a coming sunset,

In a weaver's seam,

To be picked alone,

In a shimmery dell, whatever was awakening,

For in the forests there they dwell,

Two filled circles,

Amicable Nymphs,

Succour and Symmetry,

A Spiritual Plinth.

2

The Gypsy Police

The Gypsy police were the common travellers with an eye for the law regarding traffic and the roads, they were in the ballerina's lights in the ballet orchestrated by the directors of that performance, who, just as it happened didn't care for most of them. They all had a Travellers tan, that of a well hewn complexion swarthy skinned and eagle eyed. Marcus was such a man, 5'11" dressed in khaki combats and driving a Mitsubishi Shogun 4x4, he'd rented it from an old friend for a week for £100 and was driving intently on the one track rugged roads.

Sit with the spirits in a draft and youll get a Travellers Tan.

Help comes in many forms, that of a crow that of the worms, if the worm you choose or the Faery Fly the Midges the mushroom or the tree the spirit of consciousness is seldom shared with an Anum Charra. He had few friends and fewer enemies but what he had left at the side of the road was Attachment.

It was an unofficial operation, a medium strained the atmosphere and was hell bent on sacrificing the front of the label on his branded bottle of Barefoot wine as Boydie had a strangle hold on his own mind, the medium corresponded with a scaffolder from Finglas Dublin who told the medium he was right in his way of thinking....

She earned her keep from salvage from the midst of an island crew

Till the sweet strained embers followed

Leaching and leaving nothing but the view.

As she laughed in the lay by of life's wake she touched the feeling of the tribulations corners that mean more as you get older and say a blessing for the happiness in the direction you have come...

Maggi continued "Where did the old ways get us, but to hiding in ditches and valleys when the multitude of sins are being committed in the open, not beside the hearth fires do we dwell but in the Temple through the bars of Golgotha and Streatham, in Buckna and in Galway and beside the old onion headed managers who maketh a man with merriment in the crumbs of his tea leaves go awry. And so, yet we will continue to doff our cap to the system which engendered us and give birth to an untested advance in the culinary sciences."

Coinneach replied "May the scent of lavender sooth any cares from the blessed path you may walk and may the ringing of harebells, the dancing of the Spriggans and the howl of a lamenting bull elephant. toll the days and nights of your contentment,"

"To Rely on the ancestral visions that ensure a thread of spiritual obscurity even if it means something altogether different to the others of the same ilk, is to fry your brain with the heart sap of a living Willow." Maggi said, She relayed a thread that unspun like the thought she had been given from the silence between his words and saw the world through the eye of another gold-plated executive of the devil's commandments.

That morning Teresa the barmaid chided him that if he was going to order a coffee every 10 minutes that he could think again, she wasn't in the mood,

"don't you have any coffee where you are living" she chirped

"I do but I don't mind giving money to somebody else for it"

"well in that case ill put you a pot on"

The universal Grandfather's omen of the dusty blood red Moon, in sight of which, he teased the coir, the umbilical cord of mutual connection and symbiotic attraction... Essentially all was well with his amble through the freedom of Ushet lake and the ensuing Ramble had left him dry and drab and thirsting for a torrent for the Currach, One where the arid deserts of majestic hand-maidens would have a fly past encounter bar maid style, and accompany his intuitive stride. Where the Magik of the volcano like oasis would appear and deliver the gifts he had sacrificed for the resurgent relatives of the Fae and the Sidhe,

The excitement of the freshly harvested field left her inconsolable, he had the seed for the next years crop but no tractor so he determined to use the hand sewen fiddle method, all that was left undone could wait until he had formed the mashed potato and scallions into an effigy of the statue of liberty with the aid of some Golden cow butter....

They walked towards the gate of the upper middle field and stopped at the corner beside the old stone wall ruins, your pocketful of cotton rags for my rusted racing bicycle she proffered, he was mesmerised by the sharp pain to his calf and ankle as he watched his friend drag a log from the ditch toward the gate. None of this matters he pondered as he made his way limping towards the Ox Bow Lake the other side of the wall.

Coinneach broke the stem of the Ragwort as he watched the panther slip in the gate, he reflected on his days toil and determined to forgo the necessity of his beliefs insistence that there was only one true God, for he had found the garden pleasing and the panther no danger to his existence so why would he pray other than to placate a religion that in no way found him perfect, the mirror of hope that he held in his gaze was the Pagan mother Earth, and its origins were irrelevant.

After the mischievous pursuit of infamy, he rested his heals on a bar stool in Madisons on Botanic Avenue Belfast, the aftertaste of the bitter Turkish coffee was the only thing that reminded him of the fact that he was in company, albeit isolated from driving rain that had pursued him all day. The only thing that separated him from the wino who sat on the step outside Oxfam on botanic avenue was the bottle of red wine and the glass into which he poured the bottle resonated with a style and a guile with which he was surely accustomed…

The Grass is only greener because the shits deeper. Boydee

When the dust of determination sweeps across the nation, the loose ends are getting fewer I'm wanting to tie it down? When self doubt and self worth are not on the agenda you create your own eddy all that is left are the reflections of a utopian existence not to be held by one person but to be embraced and stored among friends companions and lovers.

In the stillness and solitude of an unguarded moment Maggi held aloft an empty palm and embraced the unnatural order, it was omnipotent, in the ashes of a life forged in the goals and dreams she had as a child maiden, these sat well with this moment in time that she had been gifted, She had poisoned her body and mind with copious amounts of social conditioning all that existed for her was this moment in time and that had gone, left with the party of tourists That walked across corn market, which bathed, unlike him, in the rich sunshine beside the Masonic Hall.

Self belief is no obstacle for attainment but a boon for the wisdom put away inside at the moment passed on from one to another,"

You can choose to be passive or participate, but to do it under your own terms is a way of life he chose, those terms were simple to create his own reality whilst manifesting it only during the journey not at the destination…

As one of the many few, I struggle to appreciate the beauty inherent in simplicity, this does not mean I'm at odds with the masses I just find the masses odd!

If you chose to play a part then its no part that was predestined from your ancestors….

He was swimming in clearwater Rathlin the auld lake vanishing of course beside the faery mound, moving towards a lifejacket that moved endlessly to and fro on an evening tide… there was a swell from his sunken yacht that churned up the mud of his past life from boredom and wealth.

It wasn't the spirit she was looking for it was the soul, shed settled in her ways long before long before shed set her goals.

3

Maghaberry Prison

Coinneach cast his thoughts back to Maghaberry Prison, Foyle wing and his 6 month period of confinement, Roe cell block had been the Introductory phase, new prisoners were inducted for a week and introduced to the prison regime, where he got his cell mate to shave his head with the razors they had been issued, smoking the last of his tobacco he knew remand could be a long time, as he gathered the buts from the yard where they got two one hour walks enough to gather the tobacco and stretch the legs. Roe was a blast, he shared his cell mates prescription tablets, god knows what they were but they got him out of his head and the two babbled incessantly.

Foyle wing was to be his block, he was put in a cell with a middle aged man, with a plume of smoke around the cell he put his bag on the bed and lay down with his prison issue jogging bottoms and a T shirt along with the plimsoles, the middle aged man didn't say much and that's the way it went on for a week no yard and a walk down to the kitchen where you could iron your clothes, the food was basic but was more than he had been used to, delivered to the cell door the decompression cell where he could accustom himself to his freedom being taken away from him in return for a crime of passion brought on by death threats from a friend against his ex-partner and his son, he had been close to confronting him but instead went to the police to make it known a threat had been issued and he wanted them to know about it.

The guard appeared and told him to get his belongings together which he did quickly and followed him through 2 locked doors, all he could think of was tobacco and its supply from his last cellmate, the guard opened the door and showed him his new bunk with a new cellmate, he nodded slightly and lay down with his kit at the bottom of the bed, he resolved to use his best travellers accent when the door flap was opened and another inmate told him to get out of the cell as his cellmate was a paedophile, he eyed the prisoner and said right so…He wondered how the Warders would take it with his change of accent but resolved to keep it up.

The next few hours were thoughtful in foyle wing and he only thought let he who has sinned cast the first stone,

In November he had been living in a caravan in Portrush and had bought a decommissioned AK47 from an army surplus shop in Toome. At night he would smoke his resin he had got from a trip to Galway via Dublin, he had got £1000 worth of resin but had really been looking for LSD. ....

Anyway, he had his computer and would play his music and smoke in the caravan until wasted and in the early hours of the morning go outside and play sniper with the AK47 until paranoia of the other residents would send him inside the caravan again. He had been separated from his Partner Karen and son Jude for about 4 months and had been living in the garage of his parents recording and writing his own songs and covers on a sharp minidisk player and loving it, taking walks with his tri colour border collie Murphy, who he got re-registered as Colonel Moirphy bought from a farmer in County Fermanagh. He had ordered 30 railway sleepers and got them delivered to his 1-acre field and got David the farmer who rented the field to use the forklift to take them to the corner of the field next to his house where he could build them into shape. Mornings were taken up heaving and hauling them into the shape of an igloo, using the Stihl chainsaw to cut them to length. he cut scaffold planks into 1-foot lengths and used them in-between the rows of sleepers. Moirphy was by his side all the time gnawing on a bone or chasing a ball which Coinneach would throw intermittently. It took him about 2 weeks 4 hours a day to have the structure in place. He had put chicken wire on the outside of the sleepers covering the joints and then cut grass sods and covered the structure.

4

The Antrim Tramp

That night was his celebration he gathered up his camping stove and billy cans and a packet of Koka dried noodles a can of tuna and a can of beans and sat inside with Moirphy and made his dinner. Then the two set out across the fields to the faery thorn where he said his daily pagan prayer, it was just in-between two of his grandfathers' fields beside some running water in a ditch, It was September the air was fresh and cold and he decided that a walk to Antrim castle gardens through the fields would be great for him and Moirphy and to sleep out under the stars. He grabbed his rucksack and set off through the fields with Moirphy close behind, the ground was soft at times and he noted any wildlife with appreciation and wonder opening and closing gates behind, perhaps he was practicing for another continental journey, perhaps not, he was happy to be with Moirphy and up for an adventure. They passed Whiteside's corner and into the field where the old wooden windmill still stood, he remembered that the owner who he had visited 3 years ago had said he would fund a project to get it working again but Coinneach never got around to it. Moirphy was happy chasing sticks and scouting the ground ahead occasionally chasing a hare or a rabbit which broke cover. They found themselves going further from the road the way the gates were arranged and Coinneach decided to veer back towards the Ahoghill road and walking on the right-hand side covered the miles to Randalstown, up New street and toward the Viaduct, a magnificent structure made from basalt in the 18th century, he had Moirphy on the lead as he was used to roaming freely the majority of the time and could be easily distracted. They walked past the entrance to Shanes castle the family seat of the O'Neil's and out along the Randalstown road. It was about 6pm and the rucksack was feeling heavy so Coinneach tightened the belt around his waist and loosened the shoulder straps arching his back and holding the shoulder straps forward with plenty of slack about his shoulders taking all of the weight on his hips. He had the rucksack well packed with two sleeping bags on cut in half for Moirphy noodles beans and tuna a 2-litre jar of water dry meal for Moirphy billy cans cutlery a stove Swiss army knife and a few layers of clothes. They reached Clotworthy house about 7pm and rested at the bandstand taking in the evening light and easing his feet legs and shoulders. Moirphy seemed happy licking his paws and being stroked. Coinneach brought out his stove and billy cans filled one with water and lit the gas, while they were boiling, he put out Moirphy's dish and filled up the dry mix and left him to his own devices. There wasn't anyone about and as he poured out a cup of coffee, he thought back to the time he had been a labourer at Masserene Barracks working 6 days a week12 hours a day mixing cement and attending the bricklayers, buying army boots off the soldiers and getting 3 free meals a day until scabies broke out in the hut the workers were sleeping in. So, he decided to walk around the outside of then camp after the food. He placed the noodles in the billy can and after about 10 minutes they were done so he opened up the can of beans and tuna and mixed the tuna through the noodles leaving it on the heat for a couple of minutes then he turned the gas off and mixed the beans through cold. he took out his fork and spoon and twisted the noodles on and the beans and tuna missed on the spoon. After the first bite he knew it was at the right temperature and scoffed the lot. Moirphy had finished his dried mixture and Coinneach poured out some water. He took out a small bag of sand and cleaned the billy can with it rinsing the sand out with some water, dried it with his tea towel and started to pack it all away in the order in the rucksack that he had trained himself.

The barracks was surrounded by a river and a canal for the army boats, Coinneach wondered if he could get around it or for that matter be stopped while doing so. They set off Coinneach in front Moirphy behind and rounded the first side of the perimeter with no problems Moirphy was well behaved if he went off Coinneach just said heal and Moirphy came back into line. There were cameras all around and Coinneach ignored them concentrating on Moirphy when they hit the third side where there was an inlet surrounded by concrete banks and a plinth at the top of about half a meter wide. He hadn't expected this and a flash of doubt whether Moirphy would loose his footing and fall into the canal below with no banks to climb out on, But he started off toward it anyway and Moirphy followed, he took his time and kept an eye on his own footing never mind Moirphy's. All went well and he breathed a sigh of relief as they got onto the grass again, "Good Boy Moirphy" he repeated about three times and ruffled his fur. Surley with the cameras and all there would be somebody out to see what they were doing. No Nobody came and the rounded the last corner about 8.30 and headed in the dimming light back to the bandstand. Coinneach put his rucksack down and unwound his carry mat and brought out the two sleeping bags. Opening Moirphy's up and zipping it up again after he had got in. Dawn came about six o'clock and although cold, both were in good spirits Coinneach made coffee and water for Moirphy who was scampering about the green, still no one appeared no body was about, so he packed up cleaned up and they set off towards Aointrim, about two miles later they came to a garage and Coinneach bout sausages bacon and hash browns enough for both of them. He thought about the walk home again and decided that hed try a taxi first which he rang and said there was a dog as well, the taxi arrived about 15 minutes later and soon they were home again at IOSA Upperdoon.

Looking at the railway sleeper hut he hoped to turn it into a bird sanctuary with the hut a hide to view the birds from how he would do it he didn't know, what grass, plants or shrubs or even trees would he need to plant. The house and the garage were separated by a barbed wire fence which he had to climb over, what a nuisance he thought and decided to cut the wire between two posts. He got the snips and threw the ball for Moirphy, then he cut the four strands and looped them back over the previous post. All done now he could get in and out to the hut easy without getting tangled up in barbed wire.

The next thing his father came at him shouting as he was walking over the grass about the hole in the fence, Coinneach tried to explain but his father was livid with anger,

"I'm only getting a path to the hide without having to climb over the fence for fuck sake" Coinneach said exasperated, "It's my field" he continued. Something came over Coinneach and before he knew it he placed his leg behind his fathers and pushed him over onto his back, "let that be an end to it" Coinneach shouted and stormed off into the house. Looking back it was a bright idea he had to ring the police, but rang them he did and said his father had came at him with a knife, he disarmed him and put an end to it. Within the hour the police were there and coinneach was in the hide making coffee. "Coinneach" came the shout from the policeman "Come out", Coinneach crawled through the entrance about four foot high as the policeman asked him if he had any sharps. "Just my knife" he replied, "come down to the van", as Coinneach followed he saw another two policemen with his father. After half an hour or so the other car drove off and he was arrested on Assault and taken to the police station where he stayed in a cell for two days before being taken to Coleraine court house and placed in a cell. He told his solicitor his version of events and said he didn't want to press charges and in front of the judge it was decided that his father would live in the house and Coinneach the garage and that no further action would be taken.

Coinneach sat and listened to the ticking of the clock, he had the teapot on the boil on the 4 ring camping stove, every morning he rose opened the window peed in the sink put on the coffee and then put on a record, it was a 2 record edition of Winston Churchills speeches, everything was wired up to the stereo system and then into and out of the computer via the optical system socket. Days were a dreamland walking Moirphy up to the Faery Thorn and reciting his Faery prayer, afternoons and evenings spent with Moirphy walking the fields or in the garage playing guitar or piano and recording what he was singing on his sharp minidisk player and editing it on his computer using soundforge. Some of it was stream of consciousness making sure to have a start middle and end. His two favourite of that type were:-

1. I'll Vouch For (I am I for they are they) and
2. The queens shilling

I'll Vouch For (I am I for They Are They)

And I'll vouch For Saliva

And Ill Vouch for a head on your shoulders

And I'll Vouch for Saliva, And I'll Vouch for saliva,

And ill vouch, For The Dead,

And I Slept by Brookside

And I slept in a plastic bag

And They say I went walkies

And They Say, in Death

Turnover

Turnover

And Its Clear Now when your all alone

Driving or walking down the road

For its clear now when your walking

And its clear now in death

Don't sell your marriage bed,

keep it where your wed

Don't split up don't talk about

Get The money first.

Get the money first

Get the money First

Buy A Ticket just youse two

Get the relations to go too

Pay for nothing do what you like

They already knew it

Spike my drink sir please

Talk to him over there he has me money

Talk to Her Over there she stole me wife

Talk to them over there they're looking funny

Ive a bomb and she's a knife. (blade)

Take her to the moon and bring her back

Feed her all the drugs you can and fill your rucksack

If she goes to work give her nothing

Spike her drink when she comes home.

Keep her close never far away

Tell her sister you're the IRA

Tell her brother hes a unionist

Tell her mother your having a bad day

Buy a gun and decommission

Buy a gun and chop it up

Take to drugs not drink in coffee

Clean your floor with a wooden cup

Beat her with a wooden spoon till she's so happy

Till the welts come outta her arse

Give her hugs and dry her nappy

Take her to the moon and buy her gorse

The Queens Shilling

There was a young cowboy dressed up in white linen

Dressed up in white linen as sweet as the day

He Willed? His eye downwards, And left his thigh downwards

As he slopped though the slap of that same day

And he flew away brightly one evening

For No Hope in this land could he see

Me Life has been wasted and now ive been tasted

And now its time to go me own way

Never say never again

Never turn inwards when backwards will do

Fer im on me own so they say

And fer all the dead children who never came out

Would it be better to stay in or to leave to go out

Fer were all for war, and were all for pay

But never say backwards

when your on your way

Avaaaaaant Of Youth, For free ill point out Sandy Row

And The Day They shot you on the bridge they say

Was Only one for you,

But why you call round when theres stout in the pint

And now theres room in the pound

Never say backwards, when your on your own

A jab or a yab sure she'll do

For now were playing and down for the hay in

And hello how d'you do

For the old days are back now but backwards well stand

Down the wrong way in your own foreign land

So Never say never again

And a fifth or a seventh or an eighth when we stopped

A Cup or a yap or a drop

For who gives a damn when your only half living
Muckin out the auld slop.

Never say never again,
For your on your own when you've got the yen
For you take the queens shilling will you take the queens knife
and stuff it up yer arse with a yap.

For the police died for nothing for 60 years, old
We shot one for one 2 for 2
And now that were living this dead life we owe
To no man not even a how d'you do.

So whats on your mind now, well im not that sure
Have you much on the day no I aint
Now that were downwards well stand our own way
And one will be our count.

5

The Whales Tale

It was 1992 Coinneach and Marcus were living in Portrush, Marcus had just returned from Amsterdam and Coinneach had called to see him at his parents house, Marcus was up to high Doo talking about his time abroad and what it was like returning to this house. Coinneach had been working as a labourer for Henry Brothers Magherafelt doing security contracts, Police stations, court houses and Army Barracks. He had been working with a steel erector Ian, who 2 years earlier had been shot by the paramilitaries in an ambush while Ian was driving collecting the workers. Ian had told him he had stopped at a different place than usual and then the gunmen appeared through the hedge and sprayed the van with bullets, he pulled out his PPW personal protection weapon, handgun and tried to fire back but it wouldn't fire, later he would figure out the safety was on and in the panic, he had forgot to disengage it. He drove off to the screams of the other men in the van and made it to the hospital. This was only the start of his ordeal, during the statement to the police they told him who the men were who had carried out the attack and where they came from, and also told him that now he was a danger to others and that they had to take his PPW away from him. During his recovery his wife told him he had changed and that she no longer loved him and wanted a divorce and that he could no longer stay at his home. This sent Ian into a rage and anger even more so than the shooting, there had been an appointment made with a Psychiatrist after which he was sectioned under the mental health act.

When Coinneach met Ian, it was at Antrim Courthouse, Ian had been brought to the site as the steel erector and Coinneach was to be his labourer, Ian stayed for a day and inspected the plans and where all the steel was stored, he said it was a mess, a disaster and told the site agent that and that he wasn't going to do the job and left the site. This left Coinneach and the site agent told him he was now the steel erector. It was a living on site job and Coinneach didn't mind. He looked at the plans and couldn't make any sense of them so every day for a week he climbed to the top of the structure and sat and looked at the plans, came down for his meals and listened to his CD player to put him over to sleep at night. On the Friday of his first week the PSNI informed the site agent and him that he couldn't work up there any more as he was being targeted for an attack a shooting from the car park buildings opposite. On Monday morning he was transferred to a dockside warehouse being built in Coleraine where he was to work with Ian who had been given the job. Ian talked of how unhappy he was at work and felt that Jim Henry owed him, owed him more than the danger money he was getting paid, he said that after this job he was going to go out on his own and take on work. Coinneach said he was going to go back to university at the following September, he had been accepted for an engineering degree and that from now to September he would work with him, it was June. When the warehouse had finished Ian said that he had work in Portrush and he had rented a flat and did Coinneach know any plasterers, Coinneach said he would ask around.

And so Coinneach called to see Marcus who was a plasterer, and after Marcus had finished his rant about living back home and his time in Amsterdam Coinneach told him that he had a job and an apartment in Portrush starting on Monday if he wanted it. Marcus was over the moon and rolling another joint said, "I owe you big time for this".

They met Ian at the flat in Portrush on Sunday, it was on the first floor opposite the Londonderry Arms a one-bedroom flat which Ian was paying for. Ian had brought two six packs of Harp and chatted to Marcus whilst drinking the cans, Marcus rolled away at joints and unpacked his rucksack as did Coinneach who took the bedroom as he was the one who had organised the work. Ian was in a controlled jolly mood as was Marcus and the pair kept the craic going till about midnight. The next morning Ian took them in his green Ford escort to a large shed about a mile away and said this was to be their work for the next couple of weeks, clearing it out and renovating it. It was jam packed with rubble and rubbish which the pair cleared out into a trailer and took turns with Ian emptying it at the local dump. Nights were spent in the Londonderry arms lounge with craic and Guinness chatting with the locals and tourists alike and getting hammered on Captain Morgan's rum. Ian paid well and every Friday on time. When the shed was cleared out Coinneach tended Marcus mixing plaster and clearing up after him. Ian would always talk about how much Jim Henry owed to him and how he would get even with him. Next job was the Londonderry Arms taking off the old plaster and re-plastering it. It was July and there were lots of day-trippers and holiday makers and as they filed past the cordon Marcus's boom box rang out endless reggae songs and eased the toil of the day.

Next they went to Portstewart a simple job skimming out a kitchen extension and building back door steps in Portstewart, The radio had been on the day before whilst they were working announcing that a whale had washed up dead on the strand, Marcus suggested they should go for a look at lunchtime, so when lunchtime came they jumped in the Coinneach's grey Skoda Octavia and off they went, they arrived to massive queues each paying £5 per car for entry onto the beach, they duly paid and parked up on the beach, when they went over to the huge dead carcass there were children climbing over it and no protection of the whale no cordons and no National trust staff, Marcus said,

"Between low tide and high tide there is no law to who can claim the whale as in salvage rights"

"that's a good one so we in theory could come and take the whale", Coinneach said.

"That's right Coinneach, lets get out of here and get back to work" Marcus Laughed.

They spent the rest of the day finishing up the interior of the room and got back to Portrush about 6.30 pm, it was Friday and the weekend was ahead of them. They showered and cleaned up the flat for Ian coming at the weekend and in case they might bring any girls back for a party.

The Londonderry Arms was all hustle and bustle as they pulled up a chair at one of the Lounge tables. Two pints of Guinness and 2 Captain Morgan's rum were accompanied by a plate of garlic wedges and 2 plates of battered cod and chips. Marcus said he had been on the phone to one of his friends and they were talking about the dead whale and his friend said that the only way an individual whale could be identified was by its tail, and Coinneach said wouldn't it be good to make a cast of the tail and have it as an educational piece for the schoolchildren, something positive could come out the situation. They both agreed over their drinks that that would be a great idea. They moved to the bar and continued with the Guinness and rum, sent drinks over to a couple of girls who said thankyou but they were waiting for their boyfriends. Marcus was really happy that everything was going so well and that he had another chance to get himself on his feet. Coinneach told him no thanks was needed and that he was happy to help. The bar had cleared somewhat and they were both talking over old times when a man sitting beside them at the bar joined in the conversation, to and fro the conversation went between Marcus saying "Is that right" and "well did you know" between the strangers observations and stories. When the stranger started talking about security building work and how the people shouldn't be doing that Coinneach piped in with a few sarcastic remarks never bellying that that's what he had been working at for two years previously. Soon things got out of hand and glasses were smashed and the stranger and Coinneach were brawling on the floor. Marcus intervened and broke the two up saying it was time for home. So they both had a double rum for appearance sake after Coinneach had apologised for the mess and headed home. It was about half eleven and again they had had no luck with the women. So Coinneach decided he was going to look up a call-girl. He found an advert in the local ads section for an escort at £100 an hour. He had had no luck with any girls since his last relationship broke up and had decided that this was his only way of getting rid of his "dirty water". He rang up Suzi in the ad and she said she was available and would be around in half an hour. Coinneach told Marcus what he was doing and offered to let him have his turn at no cost, Marcus said he wasn't interested but that Coinneach could plough away.

Suzi arrived at the flat with a bodyguard who after meeting Coinneach said he would wait in the car. She came in and asked if she could take a shower after Coinneach had showed her the bedroom. She came out of the shower five minutes later and jumped in the bed with him, put a condom on him and asked if he wanted anything special, he said up the bum and she said she would have to see his size first. Coinneach tried to kiss her but she said no kissing and then he fondled and kissed her breasts and entered her and was going for about forty minutes when she tried to finish him off with oral sex, it wasn't working and she said she shouldn't do it be she took off the condom and finished him off with her mouth. He paid her and left her to the bodyguard and after chatting with Marcus again over a can of beer retired for the night.

Next morning was Saturday Coinneach and Marcus were up early and were chatting about the night before when Coinneach had a brainwave, why dint they go to Portstewart Strand early and take the tail of the whale and get a cast made, Marcus laughed and said that would be a great idea. They both jumped in Coinneach's car and made their way to the renovation job where they picked up an old plasterboard saw and a few dust sheets, when they got to the beach they paid their £5 at the entrance and drove up to the whale, there were about a dozen onlookers round the whale and Coinneach marched straight up, Marcus on the other hand laughed and said good one Coinneach, Coinneach went ahead with the plan and started cutting off the tail, while Marcus started talking to the onlookers saying they were official workers doing a job, it was hard going and Coinneach called Marcus over to take a turn at the cutting, whilst Marcus tried to calm the ever increasing and agitated onlookers, they swapped over twice more before the job was finished, cutting through the cartilage was the hardest, but finally Coinneach laid flat the seats and the boot compartment of the Renault 19, and they both hauled the tail into the back of the car. About 3 foot of the tail hang out the back. They jumped in the car and Marcus tied a rope onto the tail and said "let's get out of here". They drove up the ramp out of the beach and headed towards the country side, Marcus was sure there was an unmarked police car behind them so Coinneach put the foot down. They travelled the back roads to Antrim where Marcus had a friend an artist Lenny a sculptor who lived on a farm and Marcus said would help them. They arrived at Lenny's place at about 3 o'clock in the afternoon and knocked on the farmhouse door, his wife answered and told them he was in his workshop, they walked up a small path next to the hayshed and Marcus Knocked the workshop door out came Lenny, "great to see you Marcus, what have you been up to" greeted Lenny,

"Were looking you to give us a hand out, come and see what we've got," said Marcus

They all walked down the path and came to the car,

"What in heavens name are you' s at, is that the whale's tail from Portstewart that's all over the news on the radio," said Lenny

"yes, that's the tail and were going to make a cast of it and eventually display it at an exhibition or at schools and I was wondering if you'd help us out", Marcus went on

"well it will cost a couple of hundred for the fibreglass and the resin, so if you' s will get all that sorted then I'm in, on one condition that nobody finds out that I was involved" replied Lenny

"your on" Marcus replied.

Upon their return to Portrush they found Ian waiting and told him all about the saga, he said he'd been listening to news bulletins all day, but he had an interview with a reporter to go to in Coleraine about his time with Henry Bothers and the shooting and would the pair of them come along as he had a bad feeling about it. So off all of them went and arrived at the prearranged car park where Ian saw the car he was meeting and Coinneach and Marcus came along. They jumped into the car and as soon as they had said hello the woman said "I'm DI Freeman and I'm arresting you for blackmailing a government official". Ian's hunch had been right and the boys said tthat it was nothing to do with them and that they were leaving, the DI said no problem and they were back off to the flat. Their job had finished for now and Marcus was getting bored with Portrush anyway, but they stayed on in the flat for another month

6

He's My Husband, A Stop Gap For An Evening

It had been an emotionally charged day 20 coffees drank over 5 flask refills, his money now was rationed to £20 which had to last him until Friday and it was Monday, he was by Ballycastle beach bay Harbour Inn. At the bar a woman gave her child a coke, A mothers eyes look through to the soul, a brick wall and a cross were the only stable things present he mused.

A Muslim in a Hijab walked past and Coinneach said Shukran he replied hows she going Coinneach scratched his head and put another roll up in his mouth when Maggie just out of sight rolled up in a taxi and hid behind the harbour wall to check out the bars clientele. Maggi squinted at the ladybird who was cleaning its wings, she had packed up her belongings into her rucksack and army satchel which was hung over the ends of the rucksack frame down her torso.

So Coinneach walked into the lounge at the bar Maggi still had him under wraps and no one seemed to remember a year ago when he was forcefully removed and barred, the jazz band drank bottled water and Coinneach gestured to the barmaid who remembered his black coffee, wandering whether he had any sugar left in his right pocket. He let loose the black tar of McAlpine steam before up the road the roller driven by a lazy man followed a navvy who was paid twice his wage was Convalescing at the marine hotel.

Curses Are like chickens they always come home to roost, the bouncer remembered him and gave him his marching orders grabbed him by the arm and marched him through the games room giving him a slap on the side of the head It was one more than was needed as he fell face down into the pool table, covering his ears and planting a blow on his attacker who flinched but continued to throw him out the back door.

He sat in the old back yard and unlocked the gate which led to his sleeping quarters for the evening, he counted his money piling it up on one plastic fiver, 2 pound coins 2 50's 2 20 pence's two 10's and a one, the bark of a long haired Labrador retriever interrupted his counting, my days on a 3 year rolling retreat are over.

The sea in the distance gave him a goal his skin was now laddered about his eyes and his jowls were beginning to form, it was June 11th and the best of the summer was ahead of him, that what mattered most, a Volkswagen caddy 2 TDI bright red pulled up at the side of the cutting.

7

The Foot Of The Hill

As I walk over the field to greet the faery lore

I spy a trail made by the sheep and the sword

All dressed up in me waders I never stood still

I dreamed of the saviour at the foot of the hill

For me name it is Coin and my grip is real tight

Im sitting up now for the dead of the night

To cloak meself up and to never stand still

To dream of the saviour at the foot of the hill

So looking for company I turned to come down

I felt every footfall as me heals hit the ground

Afraid to go under I held on with a will

And waited for the saviour at the foot of the hill

A horse drawn cart, a butterchurn

A stationary wagon

The journey to learn

[Lets cut to the chase]

We focus on a new direction

Not just for any cost

For to alter our perception

Trying to get back what we lost

Thumb in the Palm means stop think listen.

The house of Beauty Mother Earth cannot distinguish between

its own perceived reality and that which is in the old poems

stories & songs hidden in the annuls of time immemorial itself.

One for the long finger, a bracelet betrothal

8

Chapter 2

She was meely mouthed and Marcus knew it, she said nothing that didn't mean no, now was the time to get her on his side, grow the spuds and make plans for the year ahead, the song rattled in his head move along Get along, move along get along, go move shift

[Maggie]
I laugh when things are dangerous
Get google to translate
Our love will come in a mother tongue
For not just milk goes out of date

Marcus washed lazily that morning Nerak was coming to the house, in fact she was there already, he sparked another pure grass joint and lay back to let the saints take care of the ether in which he was feeding. The five fresh daffodils still lay in his hat given by Coinneach as a donation to his cause, he flicked his hair down and wandered how he would get on the good side of Maggi, he rolled his stash for the day and wondered who the daffodils were for.

Funds were low, borrowed to the hilt, the powerful underbelly of Ravenskull (Nostrils) a strong hold is developing dipping my toes in my heritage, a place where time is fluid not linear,

There was more writings on the Laptop hard disk he had to find them he scrambled furtively over the bed where the ginger tom who forgave him the assault that had been. he had to find out more about the stag.

John Kennedy was holding the shop together, free as a bird and light as a feather, Martin had half his breakfast that morning, I had none but then the thoughts turned to the ashtray I could make if I ate out of the Tuna can my bowels raged and with no pressure at all I made it to the newly furbished kitchen.

As he noticed the plain scone Nerak had placed on the bird tray where martin the Raven had ate 32 Peanuts, the conversation turned to Lucky Liz, Sparky and Amanda

I cant sleep my lifeblood has been disabled, birds fly away at lightening speed and the snows of the English legal system are nearly upon us, only Mary Lee is offering uncorrupt channels though somewhat broken by the event horizon, would I survive my pure and waking dream. Flocks of Herons fly in the shade of the sandbars pike removed traces of the half eaten flesh of mink and monk fish... the berries not for human consumption were the tracers of a bygone race the Tuatha de denann.

The Tuatha de Denann had been summoned to play Marcus's game, the words were important, very important but the medium man, 6' 16 stone that carried them was only a Reflection on the Mirror. He was ahead of the sunset by two hours the ship had sailed at dawn but within 24 hours there was to be fire.

He was breathing easier having slept for 6 hours but how would he keep it going, the street worker why couldn't he remember their names was it because they remembered his or read into the theory that God was omnipotent the Tuatha were alive and well but

After a bit of tooing and frowing he found all he could ever want beside an old oil tank littered with dockins and debris at he top LHS of yhe Nostrils bus station. 1 hour away he would walk to the courthouse at 9 or so, John had texted him that he would see him at 8.20 plently of room for the 9 oclock walk to the courthouse, but the old building still haunted him just like the mall at College.

It Somewhat annoyed his being asked to smoke out the back, St Vincent do Paul beside the Hat-field was another solution to buying back the waistcoat he had given away, strike while the iron is hot, but his dreams told him that Eve had removed the operating system from his computer, Billy King had saved his life his lungs and his sanity and needed sanitary towels for a prolapsed arse he had thought it was his prostate but still his mind drifted back to the Masons, should he join for the still rivers run deep [Always hold a hostage], would he meet Philip again the ships captain

It had been quite a day he wrote and Rewrote the same passages, but the Jehovah witnesses in West Belfast one English had given him a tenner for his book after he announced the Republican [time for freedom] and the death warrant he hadn't asked anything but had he eaten 3 diazepam two painkillers and a tin of fatha beans in his bag but that was one for the book, why join sinn feinn he was asked, he had split himself and followed a wizened path of silence, walking the coastal path to Cushendall, he checked safari for the usual suspects, he checked the organisations and found Ar nDraiocht Fein, A druid fellowship a pagan Pantheons of what life and luck had brought him...

Tiocha Ar La, our love will come he quoted Billy King, Mickey Allen had been round earlier but he had missed him as he slept off the stress of the day, Billy slept well his lungs easing after he banned all non essential smoking in the house for the sake of COPD his inhaler ran out so he would remind him early on to get sugar and a script from Dr Singh.

The signs were all right, night came an hour after the dawn and magik filled the air, Martin the crow let the Ravens feed their brood, so warm tucked away the folly of school now, what was on the agenda next... a text.

He's me Housband

He was thinking of Ivy, the wind the rain and hidey holes as he hunkered down avoiding the Faery Thorn Billy King had planted, he dug it up.

He wrote the message/text with hands shaking as the 131 from Ballycastle,

Waines fed, Martin for breakfast, so boiled suet and cabbage and bacon for Culcannon.

I am an old man who never knew he had paced himself till, he found his tribe and was owning all he ever had, that which he gave away, with a tear in his eye he texted Michelle and wrote it down in his black Moleskin notebook, bringing himself round with a saying, its nice to be but is nicer being, oh just catch yourself on just take the time for a pee.

[For A Spell]

Oh faery lord oh faery king

As I stand inside your faery ring

Those who know not their own pace

Do not belong in a kindred place

Blessed be the children well

I only came here for a spell….

The reply came, thankyou kindly sir, my lungs are bad my ribs are broke, but im in a fine state or warmest out for my crest in Eire in Ulbster another court date so I thank you in a Alabama was for something strange

The door swung open on the half gate she rose with the foggy dew of Australia in her matted hair, She put on her face in the frosted mirror by the cobwebs of poisonous spiders, where was the WD40 the gate hinges needed oiled, in 14 years her children would see the fruits of her labour, too much yet just enough to get her to the kitchen, an incident was about to happen it came quickly enough... was it in the form of a text or just a premonition...

She had twenty dollars just enough for the WD 40 perhaps Rusty would be a good nickname for one of her children, she looked down at one pair of shoes and reclined backward onto her word processor, your only as good as the ones who love you back. "Tiocha Ar La" was shown across the heavier of the ones from Brookborough she checked the tides

9

Chpt 7 [tommy]

Irish stew at the rugby club by Ballycastle beach was provided by Tommy, Marcus had returned after leaving Coinneach to the airport closely followed by Paul who had turned up with Maggi

Rumours had been playing in her head whilst she watched Tommy hustle another pool match after the previous nights fight had left him torn and medicated and lying on his sofa at home for 2 weeks.

He had used his mothers recipe to collate the spuds 17 teaspoons of sugar coated the Roast potatoes mushrooms peas carrots and onions boiled left him with a nice starting mixture, he had had a premonition his wife was seeing another man but this didn't matter not this Sunday of all Sundays he was expecting Paul to fly in on Saturday what the hell was going on.….

Ill keep an ear to the ground …. An eyes to the stars, pray for some guidance and a tattoo fresh from the bars.

Writing was becoming such a chore he preferred the ones he recited or told in his mind, but then again they came back in their own good time. They were travelling to the dark hedges in his mind, the driver talked with his hands to say no more how would Paul be when he arrived this Friday,.

Mickey Allen reached 51 two days previously he hadn't had any romantic envolvement in two days, the spark of old flames flickered and died butter couldn't melt the anguish, it was Friday the 12th, he knew that, the RCD he put on Keidi's hairdryer was a mark of his days as a H&S officer for Coleraine DVLNI offices, the car liscensing dept of NI, sex was far from his mind and he only ever rose to the occasion when Keidi would put the stars, ledgers and transoms on the scaffold bay, the spark of life was dwindling like the leftover detritus of a dead salmon on the twisted and stony paths of Rathlin bird sanctuary, he handed Keidi a ferry ticket & a hotel booking for the Manor House his zippo had worked better since filling it with methylated spirits, lighting from a clipper if the ether / atmosphere was good, lighting from the zippo if the atmosphere was in need of a change:- he rubbed both eyes wakening up and inspected both his silver rings…. His second cup of coffee came quick, it was 3.20 in the nostrils

The Scotia stripped the Nostrils of all of the copper oxide, the auld pipes lay in the cupboard out the back the iphone was charging the Dinner lay on the bed and the speakers were beside the cupboard…

It was only Tuesday but in Williams book it was Friday, he was three days ahead of himself an investor in the afterlife now he wouldn't to be in Johns head, in the absence of any further orders

Wakening up with a spiritual sky

The crows flew out of the house

Freeing his frozen hands from the phone he humped a boulder, Sparky sat to rest on the sitting stone, alone he began to pray, "let me listen to the rhythms of the land"

The tabby ate the peanuts unsteady on its feet choking at the bit for large lumps of cow shit covered bobbys hands as he picked up his phone to talk to coinneach, a catholic priest launched a tirade at the congregation…gathering the final pages from his sermon Blind dog Ross cut a fine figure burning a match to setting on.

The cat tabby Prayed on his hind legs stretching the fur loosely draped beside Harbour hill Atlantic drive, As he passed the diamond he stooped to pick up a butt ….

You gotta bring somebody with you when your going through the levels

Rising up slowly from a hurricane from safety to destruction

To ride a level plane.

Success depends upon expectations if they are low enough failure can be deemed such.

Be careful what you wish for, for the world conspires to make it come true.

[The Auld Copper Bracelet]

Was worn till it tarnished and left its mark
On the healed it could then be shone up
Like a new brass pin and

Passed on or

Sold for auld coin.

[Red Jotter]

Coinneach sat in a clearing his rucksack and guitar stacked against the rotting framework of an old cabin, he lifted the guitar case and brought out his new Martin guitar, it had been 3 months he had been travelling alone in the open wilderness that was the North coast of Ireland he wished for companionship but held onto the thoughts of isolation and abandonment of social values, he had three days supplies of noodles and beans left with a few cans of tuna,

I dug a hole in the Afterlife

And tied a rope all around

But the dead did not wait for me

Whilst the living made few sounds

Of comfort for a changeling

Of silence that did abound

For fragrant flowering lavender

So I sat still and frowned

Sitting still made no sense to me

From the pain of moving I found

An ocean floor that spread like whores

From another nation underground

So frills and lace can fill my space

And leaflets growth does abound

For now a quill and a moonlit hill

Where I can pray at a faery mound

A wild beach hedge, A dog rose in bloom

Leaving behind, Shadows on jupiters moons

Connecting the earth to live, Spirits by a bee

A bed of leaves laid in dew, A simple goal guided by thee

The wasteland was strewn with the bodies of dead hares and dappled brown baby starlings, the mule wound its way down the forest path as a sprinkling of ash coated his trenchcoat, Coinneach parted the brambles which drew blood from his soft hands

The lake was slow and easy, a posh hotel was the setting / venue for a day after the night before, he rallied his tangled thoughts and sat bedraggled in the foyer looking out on the coastal view, locals from the Nostrils, a disembodied spirit, Avatar,

Definition was vague, all encompassing but feint in its spell on this side of the ocean, America was in the grip of a lull in its GDP

The pansies rode the wind and held his dark thoughts at bay, the ongoing turmoil of being and the myriad of lavish meadow grass that captured the essence of a spiritual life led him to pluck the daffodils and make a daisy chain, he minded "hold on" by Tom Waits as the daisy chain formed the end of a sundial, he used his compass to mark N, S, W and east....

The VW Caddy held four people 2 dressed in leathers with Rorrim on the back, an old stylised man kneeling pointing to a tuft of green grass etched in the make and at the bottom Boston, they seemed familiar to him but as they brought out the shotguns his heckles raised and goosepimples ran wild two shotguns one sawn off and the other full length they ejected 4 cartridges between them and popped in four more, thankyou kindly mam they said to the front seat passenger as they climbed in the field next to him

[For Maria Lourdes De Vera]

Although my coils have protected my essence from errant ways, I'm happy because I'm getting a closer harmony with my thoughts. I'm able to write because most of what I have experienced I have more or less kept in tune with.

She perforated the layers of her kind

For a sequence of life to be cleansed

And lay down the foundation

Of a moment in time

Making sense for them to end

The chimes closed about her heals

The bells between caught her whole

And made a familiar tingling

Of a stream her life had stole

Now a frequent visitor to the ivy that entwines

Her hands with lavender bewitched

Never to be smelt whilst time

Tied up her latest plateau

Newly dried on the line

Now with her cares laid out

Though you cleave behind

Now to lay down your head

A foundation of your kind

To drink in the atmosphere with my Anum Cara wasn't an effort, he didn't believe the world we inhabited existed and had developed a solid philosophy. He was five feet 10 and wore black dungarees with a furred pair of black mountain boots and a white peeked cap with Alabama 3 scribed on the front, he had created a tribe of 13 girls and had just turned 50 and approached a brick wall of impepertuity with a stoicism beyond his childhood training. He had helped me loose my greed that had plagued my days and Knights of fortune took its place

In a moment betrayed by none

The bright black shoe tapping

Tempting all of us awake

Let us just Turn up

For the only vegetables I need

To make my spirit weep

And raise my soul up

To beg for forgiveness

Whilst being settled in your ways

Leaves me caring none the less

Always in its day

He was a natural circle, Mal was in a leather bikers jacket and camo shorts with burgundy hiking boots, he lounged over the Chinese counter with a focus that belied his intentions,

He grasped for some sense of reality as an American accent came into earshot, "never seen anything like it before" the American continued,

Down by the harbour sits
The gems of the night
Laying memories from another time
When the Magi graced my night

The gooseberries turned from green to red
The hedgesparrows feasted with their chicks
And the starlings fought with the doves
In the summer out in the sticks

Coinneach had decided to come down from the hills after a phone call from davy that he was in Ravensbeak for 5 days, he reached down the inside of a zipped pocket and lifted out a packet of grass enough to get davy started on a bender and put it in his five pocket jeans.

He tucked away his rucksack in a locker at the marine hotel and withdrew 350 from the cashpoint inside, the bar was about a mile away and he minded his favourite songs as he passed the moving throng of tourists and locals alike, he was unkempt with his hair matted and bleached by the sun, he changed his guitar over to his other hand and as he came to the memorial fountain he unhooked his hair and dunked his head into it, tossing his hair back he pulled it into shape and hooked it with a hairband, he looked and felt like an itinerant with a headful of dreams and a campsite beside the hedge he was on the hunt for his tribe... the hill took no more of his energy out of him than the furtive glances the passers-by gave him accompanied by one or two smiles and a few frowns he entered the pub by the back door as he heard the strains of davy and John in full flow.

Davy was a slight man 5' 7" dressed casually with short hair and a tinged red face and a gait that of a guard dog, he had lived a life never far from turmoil but had settled well for his 60 years, Paul Coinneach sat down his guitar and Davy eyed it up and down eager to get the craic going that was already underway.

He went and stood by the back door it was ancient a deep purple with patches peeling back two-inch scars revealing a deep green with the stays rotting at the edges he looked over at Davys table and saw two town girls stumble and take a seat beside Davy. A glass of Guinness was knocked over and spilled on Carmels trouser suit Davy said "What the fuck" and pushed his stool backward as he sang "ill tell me ma ", paul glowered at the girls and said " don't ever do that again" It was her fault Carmel the blonde said as the other wiped herself down with toilet roll.

He had seen it before and it gave him the urge for a pint of Guinness as he sang the galway shawl.

Framed in a forgotten picture here, never to be taken out in the fear, that wed both move on to another air, from lovin you with the waxen hair, but the far off stranger still has hope, for another time with yet another scope, in the shade of a lovers moon,

Davy rang the till and walked off with a hundred pounds He was in a tizzy, music ruled his psyche and the government ruled his pocket, long live the blues he roared as willy shouted "up the Ra" The brown parched leaves grew through the ivy and fir tree giving shelter to the starlings jackdaws ravens and hedge sparrows all.

No ulbster fry laid out to to greet me
In the morning sure well see

The ghost of a foreign waitress

From Romania to Hungary

My nights all my own now

In my travellers bed

Beside me my leather waistcoat

Above my lovers head

So for all I can fortell now

As focus sometimes shifts

Back to the morning Raven

As well as a heavenly lift.

2ⁿᵈ Black book

Eyes left! head right! and well leave this road behind! and well teach ourselves our own ABC,

Lay your gaze on a Thatched roofs maze, catch the glint of a sundial's signs

Though somewhat hazy, times maybe right to be guided by Orion's steady flight

To a dwelling place scented by the turf heated through peat embers through its smoke alight

Ill be woken up with me head on the butcher's block, taking loose leaf medicines you'd be none the wiser, maggots the lot of them testing turning over the auld sod their life's duty to an enhanced childlike ball 20,000 miles in circumference called Mother Earth

As thick as boar dung on the neck of a bottle

It's a marginal ornament that emblazoned the full length of Coinneach' s right forearm, he had to distinguish between the signs, advice and reality .... But the birds were definitely not enamoured with his offerings though the robin and swallows antics showed all the signs that he needed that the frivolities were to be put to bed...

I'm walking through this corridor
With knights and saints and saviours and you
And you ask me, you ask me if I'm home

Eyes left head right
And well leave this road behind
And well teach ourselves our own ABC

The intention was in his tattoo, an ornamental decoration from the book of Kells, his hair began to shape like the zoomorphic from his tattoo, what was to become of the day ahead he lay recumbent in the knowledge that not all beasts need to be tamed.

The leaves whispered that evening, he swallowed his saliva and touched his inner forearm to be reborn a serpent in the midst of the forest he sat down rolled four cigarettes and studied the form of the northern lights, in the light he touched the kitchen thatch.

Let me fulfil your sacred dreams and make up your head, your minds made up you shall rise a hue upon the day upon the stacks you shall find a cart filled up with hay.

I'm having too much fun to think, just now I looked and looked again and put on Betty Blue make up and listened, telling me that somebody also needed the food more than me, but I emptied my body of the poisons of foreign lands, beautiful,

The girls were engrossed on each others company an older woman gnawed at a plain biscuit.

[Horseman pass me by]
Clothed I shall ride bareback
Bowed by the wisdom that not all
Stallions need be tamed.

The sniffer dog worked its way up the line and as it approached him its ears perked as it stuck its nose into his groin, he grinned slightly as he looked at its female handler and said "your fucking dogs obviously in heat"

Two Garda Siochana led him by the arms to retrieve his rucksack past their female partner and then on to a small interview room where they proceeded to empty it all including the tooth paste which they squeezed empty into the bin. After a strip search, they said

"Alright where is it"

His cyst still plagued him, only Sparky sat silent in the garden pond playing dead with the fishes, his daughter hadn't made it as far as the Nostrils but the shop front was just a mirage a long-lost dream of belonging neither his new identity, he had been given nor the fact his time was fluid, he searched for his Poteen treat every daughter as if she were your own…Don't rake over cold ashes for the children the funs over, its time to work.

Me wanting a kindred soul to be filled with tobacco perfume, and then the glasses were cleared so I shaved me beard, and left with a goal of forgiveness in my soul, so now things have changed I'm getting well outta range and the whole point is not for a lovers bed, but by saving your soul, aloud in a crowd, my attention was brought to bear on a /Richmond King size cigarette burning on top of the cistern, it was eight minutes past sometime in July 2019, he reached for his mobile and separated his cash into his front two pockets and his back pocket and reached into his knapsack for the lighter fluid, he pulled out the innards of his zippo and filled it halfway through the hole in the cotton, he then drenched the rest in the methylated spirits that had been soaking up the buds, all women are my wives"

The grey neck raven inspected the diamond Ballycastle and landed on the summer seat in front of the Church of Ireland Parish of Ramoan, it liked what it saw in the travail of a hunter, seeking that fresh food was not in order for the crows that day.

[Donkey Jacket]

If you look up the road and you see something black, if it moves it's a crow if it doesn't it's a surface man.

[An Bhinn Mohr]
Passing it on does not dull this stagnant memory,
only vague chance recollects the vivid hue,
of the ones who have passed by,
spare thoughts abound in the stream of life (days),

and light a candle for those still there,

share it with those who have loitered,

then on into the cradle of Mother Earth:- Mise Eire.

Coinneach MacPhaidin 2019

"This is what you find invariably

as you wend your way through lifes

stony and somewhat arduous paths

and other highly ambient domains" Bob Speers.

You don't have to believe in something for it to exist.

Patience is a virtue posess it if you can

Never found in women and seldom found in man… Boydee

I believe in free will up to the point where you have to make

a decision.

No foreboding only a sense of fear and isolation kept him from his kelp strewn communication room, he set his compass down on an old stump which had been preserved in his atrium, his ablutions had been necessary, now he knew that, looking at the colour of the water an oily marked hue to the sheen of the beige. He wrote Ogum in the residue of the bath drain and made his way to the drinks cabinet.

It had been 3 days since a drop crossed his lips but he unscrewed the bottle of Poteen and filled the cap, flicking his zippo he lit a rizla paper and placed it in it, the rizla burned then no flame, he ran his finger over it and pulled its singed mass back immediately it was the proper stuff, he sat with a roll up in his hand and mused at the cap, Cold lonely and frosted.

He lifted the lid and threw it down his neck, no blinding flash followed no arbitrary condemnation from the bottle, but he knew that would be the last of a long day of suspense in his kind of jungle.

He tapped at the Morse key, For what we shall reap is never stitched in the silvery mansions of the transient consciousness, lay me down easy and let me untangle the wool from the fleece of the children in the borders of the mind, what is true is formed eons before it has happened and if the spirit of ancestral heritage is abided by the followers turn to leaders in a predestined orgy of beauty and reality.

With each passing day a new reluctance to elevate my symptoms above the pay gap revolution. There was no still mass no quiet calm before the storm only the whirring of the rotor blades as he took off his shirt and sat resolute in his waistcoat and baggy jeans with no socks and a pair of army boots …

His Mojo had deserted him as he threw up the contents of his stomach over the glowing sticks and decided to make his way back to the Nostrils to meet his maker.

Right hand open left thumb in palm, he watched the birds at Doon, the taxi driver took him to a remote burnt down bungalow uphill from a forest, he made a makeshift bivouac with the burnt rafters and thick black plastic from the round bales of silage.

A grey backed crow stumbled in the conifer and flew away as the collared doves flew into the space, opening. Yet rich flora and fauna landscape. He sat motionless with hands cupped and thumbs crossed with gritted teeth. He made the sound, cupped hands thumbs toward lips of an owl, and resolved his next move was to stay scthum and explore his immediate surroundings

Let our yesterdays drop like fading petals from our consciousness onto our notepads and leave a chit of perfume on our transient relationships that we may become.

No matter where you go you always take yourself with you, Let the subconscious be an apparition and the daffodils our just deserts

Four Green Almonds Sat and honestly don't think I have any love in me, I know how to make people loved, but I felt loved but I don't know how to express it, Four green almonds Sat.Sun. Mon.Tue

Blessed are the cracked for they let the light shine through

The hearth dull as the heart beats,
Still! we wait,
Not a thing sours
Our glasses
Wiping away the sweltering heat,

A flighty bird a crow,
Stooping to feed
Our signs still
Pure and able
To walk as we read

Seagulls snipe the watchtowers
Of a presbytery dull
A language still alive
At the foot of the hill.

I'm odd as bedamed, but its nice to be nice, given the circumstances id rather be odd than be acceptable, however that may change in my time of being... confess or be dammed, bedraggled and confused, over arching concerns about the climate, rectal curiosities and penis envy are all things of the past now, concern me not that I may attain unity with my work.

It was a dark morning in more ways than one, the curtains were drawn, they were drawn at the behest of the owner, to keep the light of prying eyes from shining their awareness on the landscape of devilment at Crowskull crescent. At the nostrils there had been no lack of activity, crazy predictions from the birds, collard dove Ravens and Jack Daws, (Martin and Big Beak) were holding the sanity of the place together, Martins dictation actions from the ringing of the Chapple bell @ St Patricks to the lighting of cigarettes to the hairy underbelly of the being of Mickey Allen, who had been on a bender for the past 10 weeks since notoriety with various government organisations had brought him to the brink of freedom being incarcerated at Carstairs but not before he had infected a new generation of followers.

Mickey had broken his ankle and was incapacitated for journeys longer than 10 yards, cementing the limit by going barefoot in the buff or with his dishevelled appearance of black loose fitting jeans a T shirt with a Romany broach he had made stapled for only ones who knew not to notice out loud but to take a badge of honour not to be interfered with. Two leather waistcoats one metal pop buttons to give him regulation for his poetic love life the other for his menthol tips his roll ups and lighter, adorned round his waist was an 1 ½ "leather belt holding his zippo pouch and letterman and a sheaf, 3 house keys from IOSA on a metal bracelet, a leather coat containing Passport wallet Driving Licence a full book moleskin of notes for his new book, and an iphone SE a celtic knotwork bracelet and an Irish Republican Broach both of which he was trying to get displayed at the Marine Hotel, Ballycastle, just down atlantic avenues wayward hill walk, along to promenade where he had planned to book a room

Martin sat on top of the light, and laughed Ha! I was up before you Coinneach sniped back Aye but at least I got a ride last night Martin:- but my cocks bigger than yours he said as he sloped off and jerked the last of the piss from his member. They had pipes to lay and Coinneach reached for his hip flask as Martin had flown the Coup to get the skemmel dumper in Sparkeys freshly dented red van…. Martin floored the van to the queue up Andersons town way as Coinneach slung the shutters down, the first part of the dig. Sparky had lit a small camp fire just behind the Komatsu 210 and had lunch in a halved hinged 50 gallon drum of engine oil, he lolled towards the digger and lept up into its security as he gnawed at an apple, swiping to the left inside the cab to let Coinneach know it was time to move out of the road:-

Martin was nowhere to be found so Sparky put the dig, the excavations of the muck & soil, on the side of the trench, whilst Coinneach lept to hook up the chain sling to lift the box, the trench protector, again, hooking up all four hooks facing outwards to the four corners of the box section and heavy sheet metal, to lift the box into the dig again, he sparked up a roll up and crawled up the pipe, the 4 foot concrete storm water, to get out of the road, Sparky had nearly reached the laser line as Coinneach jumped out to use the intelligent stick for soil depth, all was good in the world, limbs and digger moved in rhyme Martin arrived back with a schaemel load of stones which Sparky scrabbed and scraped off the back of it and deposited into the trench box, He eyed Coinneach as he got the long tail the navvy and the intelligent stick to line up with the laser, next the wacker, the vibrating plate, and the jumping jenny had to be slung into the trench, all was levelled with the navvy and the pipe was unceremoniously slung to meet up with the previous pipe, Sparky elevated the pipe as he swung it into place, the sling hole had been dug well and Coinneach unhooked one part of the sling from the hook as sparky pulled it through and Coinneach unhooked the sling and the bucket ready for the shaped and fashioned railway sleeper to push the pipe 4 foot concrete stormwater home, past the rubber seal to concrete which had been lubed up with clear sticky gel….

He, Coinneach then placed the laser target at the mouth of the new pipe and swirled his finger downwards indicated a pinched finger and thumb to press the wood and twist the pipe bucket to bed in the pipe all the while Coinneach dragged on his roll up till the pipe was at the right fall, another pipe in as Martin poured the gravel into the trench after the box had been shifted upwards a couple of feet until repeated the box was clear of the trench, 5 pipes a day at the andersonstown Stream diverson at the supermarket complex.

Pull tight the net curtains… shutters
Leave the blind behind
And open your hearth to a kindred mind
Leave well alone and summon me.
In the depth of the night…
For all your weighty demons

You still can fly a kite.

For me I know you do

By the way you closed the door.

My wandering days are numbered

Like the 5 upon your door...

At the Nostrils the crows controlled the status quo. Coinneach hadn't quite worked out whether it was Billy King who had instigated this or whether it was a tribal elder from the Rathlin Island who took instructions from the mainland depending on the status quo.

The hedge sparrow fledglings had turned to vibrating lumps of life open beaked begging for the leftovers from the mothers pallet.

Billy had been feeding him whole peanuts and had tried roasting them for half an hour first to make them more palatable for the humans and for the auld Llamas Fayre.

Martin lifted 3 nuts... it had been at least two weeks since he lifted 32, he sat on his honkers, haunches, Hunkered down in a 2nd WW reinactment pit at IOSA. The lane ran up the old path by the side of the hedge running in a fork to the caravan...beside the water trough and far beside the ghost of the old railway sleeper hut….. "your perception is aloof somewhat disinterested" said Coinneach

as he Pondered the why's and wherefores of learning "Grace" by Rod Stewart, they had completed their quota… pipes in as Wanky and Coinneach booked two return tickets to portrush for their summer holidays….

Coinnach lay in the back of Sparky's van with the copper the still saw the carpet bag full of tools the petrol from the still saw the slings the hooks and Sparky driving with Marcus in the front. Coinneach puffed at roll ups continuously with a heavy air of petrol fumes knocking them out and giving a silvery hue to their task at hand.

I was a leveller a bulldozer to the senses time nor tide waited for no man as the maladies of "The streets of Baltimore" Bobby Bare echoed round the van…

Sparky had written to the headquarters in Cork…

Dear Sir….

In the brine was the residue from the primordial soup, we ate culchannon and dismembered the souls of our enemies with a branch of the Rowan tree, our roots were still attached when we asked for an olive branch we found the bitter pill of Saorise had been illuminated by a tribe we no longer recognised as one of our own, a splint was the best we could do as to chop off the young offenders would be to diminish the course…!

Lend me Ossians' Well, worn of feelings,
A heart leased and worried lent,
Because of a Lady by Lake Ushet,
Left her lacework frills and went.

A livid comely Daughter Rathlins' due,
Not a changeling of thy Kind,
Well set apace for a lowly place,
Leave her lacework frills well behind.

To Thee Thine music barely finding,
The haunting seamstress strung,
A body vest of armour,
Left her lacework frills and none.

[Bye Honey I'm Sapped]

Let us not be divided like the layers of a Dickensian novel rather plant us softly and firmly in the ashes of a glowing society where

Truth and Beauty remain but fleeting nourishment for the middle masses who vote not with the Democratic stride of a solemn beat but with the demand of the Mothers Milk...

The Tuatha De Denann came out of the mists arrogant and proud, they came riding horses with Spancil Hills Flag aloft and loud

They got their strength from the Shea who lived underground, The Firbogs they called them, the bag bellies two sounds

The legend is they had a lot of hounds who did the hunting and they left down an underground well.

I hope I live to see that day when the faye and the shea will stand strong happy medium and long... to reign over us not so good on the water maybe the boat trip will leave room for the slaughter.

When your ahead of yourself things tend to get exitable, Sparky said to Francis over the phone, I need a dry store well built along the edge of three acre plot beside the Forest in Lowerdoon here he ranted, get the feckin irish to put in a price for a dry store well in the Mexican border and have it as a tourist attraction them building it, it would get the Mexicans and the Hondurans to serve their time in dry stone walling and create a habitat for the

Chinese migratory birds to nest in it get it blessed by the pope as an eighth wonder of the world, and have Alexandria Cortez do the opening to be advertised in the Boston Globe.

Coinneach rested in the Lotus position, breathing intently as no guru had suggested, he submitted to no teaching, other than that of the birds, there was no saviour in the room no muse only the dying embers of his detritus, Alexandria Cortez had barred him and his interest in Political commentary as the players comments had only grown.

The gulls were distant now, screaming at some other mans injustice flakes of ash glowed in the hearth showing up faded lines from the Sinn Feinn Pamphlet. Mickey Allen had displayed her as an Armchair Republican, her brother near having started a riot at the crows beak the year before after some internment anniversaries impromptu speech had left the nostrils bloodied and reeling.

Resting was arresting the flow of his agenda, algae in the pond and tadpoles had been nowhere to be seen this year but Lowerdoon offered a respite that had quickly taken over Sparky's psyche, he no longer read the emails and tweets from headquarters but four were starred as important as the cauldron of root vegetables boiled in the fresh spring water from the mountain he laced the pot with the spindly magic mushrooms he had gathered at the cemetery as he called it surrounded by Rowan trees for the beast of the bog to be raised from the dead. The pipes were clear the boat was launched and the still waters could be heard mirroring the stream.

Throughout the mists of time are relationships formed through a moment, opening a shift in personal ambitions to attain ones goals?

Dreams deliver obstacles to be overcome by realities as yet unfulfilled…

Im trying to climb back into the distant past to regain a spiritual adventure climbing from a watery grave with the warm rain gradually flooding my humanity, a psychometric test of endurance feeling the end in sight, but for a cowbell to lead the herder to a watering hole in the midst of a drought afraid of going over freshly trodden ground in case the hunter becomes the prey, alone alive, confounded by a truth that knows neither hide nor hair of a focus on a ramblers path to a non sensical stream of banality.

The jackdaw weeded the grass verge as Coinneach sat raging by the willowy path, he had no food for himself let alone for his erstwhile companion, he had been made homeless again by an incident involving a photograph of his daughter at the old monastery up the road, that's where his destination was for the evening camp, the jackdaw flew off in that direction and the humidity& humility hurridly followed watching out for the familiar call of the Banashee, the banshee queen Cloidhna, too early they said for the supernatural presence but he knew it was coming, he puffed on his amber leaf roll up with its menthol filter and liquorice paper, The ravens were huge round here, he muttered our Lord out loud "bloody awesome", he took the phrase in along with the freshly scented silage they were cutting in a faraway field. From peasant to pauper from traveller to the down trodden his guitar threw him off balance as he tripped on the tufts of fescue that lined the broken stone wall.

If it is in oblivion we seek succour, remember the alternative! A mindset that draws from the well of life's experience to soothe transient times…The staggered walk in a forest path that leads to the monastery fields, of fallow ground: - in the Gods we trust a well, to have a better privilege, to survey the Plaintiffs initial thoughts:- A plan.

The life, strife and the spirit was in the windfall, bejewelled by the bastions of hope who settled by the nest of Rue River which flowed seaward towards McCuiaigs. When the torrent abated it was not that of the horizon which eased the eyes, but that that once crested closer to home.

He avoided everything that was cold comfort, the queues were non existent for those, only the ravens and Martin held the keys for the Indian Lodge the Teepee and the coal scuttle sat outside with a torpid trance of graceful politik.

No one came to close proximity to the ne'er do wells, and outlandish characters that inhabited Ruecastle. To have all the Myriad of sticks that had their spirits carved by the water and the sand dishevelled as I, there was an order in them, perhaps overlooked by many the view of Fair head and the two clocks one ten past ten the other a summer hours sundial, I rested peacefully by the shore, rue river ran its merry way to feed what was left of the flock of seagulls... ahead and behind of me lay a form which intrigued the traveller. Distinct in me the clock face of fortitude.

She examined her Labia in the Marine Toilets, in the mens as she fed her catering skills with the torrid stench of the japped and well rimmed toilet bowls!! And decided that they were in need of a walk. Her Personal cavities were her raison d'etre... deserving of her full focus while winding her peril through the dark days of winter... save for the summer months when shopping and feeding her partner took over. "Sure its only an old wives tale but your Granny swore by it" her grandfather Marcus had told her. It keeps the trailer trash at bay...Pauline swept the hours aside and resumed her coffee at the Marine.

He sat cross legged by the open fire dressed only in track suit bottoms, with his soiled feet he took the full force of the flames to stir him into action, he blew the smoke and medicine up the chimney twisting his head at right angles to do so, in front of him was a bottle of Prague beer a blank canvas with a permanency etched into the watermark... a Bavarian strain of Mystic Merlin drying by the open fire where the coals slumbered in the fire pit of an open hearth and anchored the day together intact and alouf. He sketched his thoughts on the ceiling with a permanent marker, first the morse code then the phonetic alphabet.......

He looked at the roses that grew around the bird table and wondered why they were growing away from the window. the sun, the glow blossomed North whilst the rest bloomed east, he drank to ease the pain of knowing how it all should be, he was an ever-growing divergent being who refused to recognise that this world exists in any form, he was a facilitator, a necromancer and ahead of his time by about 100 years, what had brought him to this point was a series of unrelated events.

I had given up knowing for feeling 14 years ago and lived in the dream until a spirit guide woke me up at Starbucks, his presence took a year, which was my reaction time, once on an old/new path there was no stopping till the death, All was clear. To listen to the music was not to fear earthy ways but I had to remind them of the dangers in meeting the kindred spirit.

When your on your own and in the stillness you create a home but then you turn around for a Form from the sound, that surrounds your freshly painted frown that shows some spark to behold a sign, then you know it is your time.

10

[Operation Doirty Water]

He looked like a goat but it was not direction that he needed, for after all his partner was hen toed yeti, we would revile and redraw the boundaries of the Refugee camps and latch the scoundrel not the wastrel to a lamppost for feather and tarring.

Atmospheric pressure 1026 mb… the swallows fly where they're meant to be flying and this was an omen for anything goes. When the atmospheric pressure drops they have to find their own level, the level at which they fly is lower to find the flies and thus the wee birdies fill their bellies

It wasn't the spirit he was looking for
It was her soul, shed settled in her wayward ways

Long before shed set her goals

In the rarefied atmosphere she sewed a seed for him

She never once lent an ear, as the harbour lights grew dim

[Gaeltacht, Wind Speak]

[The rest! Me Own Lot]

The womb,

the skull,

the anchor & the dove,

The view from the parapet,

Reigning from above

The Gulf Of Golgotha,

Crossed forms,

tooth picks,

Awakened not by the mercy,

Of the chaffed Rowan stick,

The power of the poker,

Wrapped Paisley scarf,

Laid bare by the maker,

Coiled up and made dark,

So For all of these notions,

I stir Dagda's pot,

The hostage is the moral,

The rest my own lot...

Coinneach MacPhaidin equinox 2019

(The Hanging Baskets Of Moyle)

A lion licking a fir tree,

A stallion stretching its snout,

A Harebell with a purple boom,

A starlings beak from the water slips out...

Coinneach MacPhaidin 08/19